Gobble, Gobble, Slip, Slop

A Tale of a Very Greedy Cat

 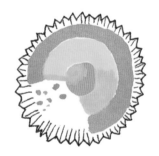 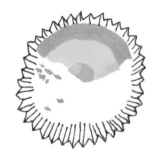

by Meilo So

Alfred A. Knopf   New York

Retold from the Indian folktale "The Cat and the Parrot," appearing in
How to Tell Stories to Children by Sara Cone Bryant (Boston: Houghton Mifflin, 1905).

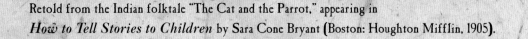

THIS IS A BORZOI BOOK·PUBLISHED BY ALFRED A. KNOPF

Copyright © 2004 by Meilo So

All rights reserved under International and Pan-American Copyright Conventions. Published in the United States
by Alfred A. Knopf, an imprint of Random House Children's Books, a division of Random House, Inc., New York,
and simultaneously in Canada by Random House of Canada Limited, Toronto. Distributed by Random House, Inc., New York.
www.randomhouse.com/kids

KNOPF, BORZOI BOOKS, and the colophon are registered trademarks of Random House, Inc.

Library of Congress Cataloging-in-Publication Data
So, Meilo.
Gobble, gobble, slip, slop : a tale of a very greedy cat / by.Meilo So. — 1st ed.
p.   cm.
"A Borzoi Book."
Summary: In this story based on a folktale from India, a very greedy cat eats five hundred cakes, his friend the parrot, the nosy old woman, and much more.
ISBN 0-375-82504-5 (trade) — ISBN 0-375-92504-X (lib. bdg.)
[1. Greed—Folklore. 2. Folklore—India.] I. Title.
PZ8.1.S6652Go 2004   398.2—dc21   2003001772
MANUFACTURED IN CHINA
March 2004   10 9 8 7 6 5 4 3 2 1   First Edition

For Ming

Once there was a cat and a parrot who decided to take turns preparing meals for each other. The cat's turn came first.

He spent the day lazing in the sun, and when the parrot arrived for dinner, the cat threw a few grains of rice into a bowl and set it in front of the parrot. After eating this meager meal, the parrot was still hungry, but he was too polite to ask his friend for more.

The next day it was the parrot's turn, and he spent the day baking five hundred delicious little cakes.

When the cat arrived at the parrot's house, there were four hundred and ninety-eight cakes waiting for him. The cat gobbled them all. Gobble, gobble, slip, slop.

Then the greedy cat grabbed the two cakes the parrot had set aside for himself and gulped them down too.

"I'm still hungry," said the cat as he burped loudly. Now the parrot was truly insulted. "There are no more cakes," he squawked angrily. "If you are still hungry, why not just eat me!"

"Yes, why not?" said the cat, and he
swallowed the parrot whole in one
greedy gulp. Gobble,
gobble,
slip, slop.

A nosy old woman saw what the cat had
done and began scolding him.

The cat gave her a mean look and said,
"I've eaten five hundred cakes,
I've eaten my friend the parrot,
and I can eat you too, I can, I can."

So gobble,
gobble,
slip, slop the cat ate the old woman.

The cat licked his lips and went along the road until he met a farmer and his donkey.

"Hey, fat cat, you better move out of our way," said the farmer, "or my donkey will kick you."

The cat said,
"I've eaten five hundred cakes,
I've eaten my friend the parrot,
I've eaten the nosy old woman,
and I can eat you too, I can, I can."

So gobble,
gobble,
slip, slop

the cat ate the farmer and his
donkey too.

The cat burped and sat down in the middle of the road. "I'll just take a little nap and then be on my way," he said.

But his nap was interrupted by a royal wedding procession. The sultan and his bride rode on an elephant, and beside them marched the sultan's soldiers.

"You best move along, Mr. Fat Cat," said the sultan, "or my elephant will trample you."

But the cat did not move.
"I've eaten five hundred cakes,
I've eaten my friend the parrot,
I've eaten the nosy old woman,
I've eaten the farmer and his donkey,
and I can eat all of you too,
I can, I can," said the cat.

So **gobble, gobble, slip, slop**

the cat ate the sultan and his bride
and the soldiers
and even the elephant.

Now the cat was so fat he could hardly move.
So when two crabs came scuttling along the road
and said, "Out of our way, fatso, or we'll pinch
you good," the cat just laughed.

"I've eaten five hundred cakes,
I've eaten my friend the parrot,
I've eaten the nosy old woman,
I've eaten the farmer and his donkey,
I've eaten the sultan and his entire wedding procession,
and I certainly can eat two little crabs,
I can, I can."
So

gobble,
gobble,
slip, slop

the cat ate the two crabs.

When the crabs landed in the cat's belly, they could see nothing.
It was pitch-black. But what a noise they heard!

A parrot was SQUAWKING.

A donkey was BRAYING.

BANG

An elephant was TRUMPET[

And people were **SHOUTING** and *crying* and **MOANING.**

And everyone was **BUMPING** and *tumbling*

NG.

OUCH

BANG

OHHH

against each other!

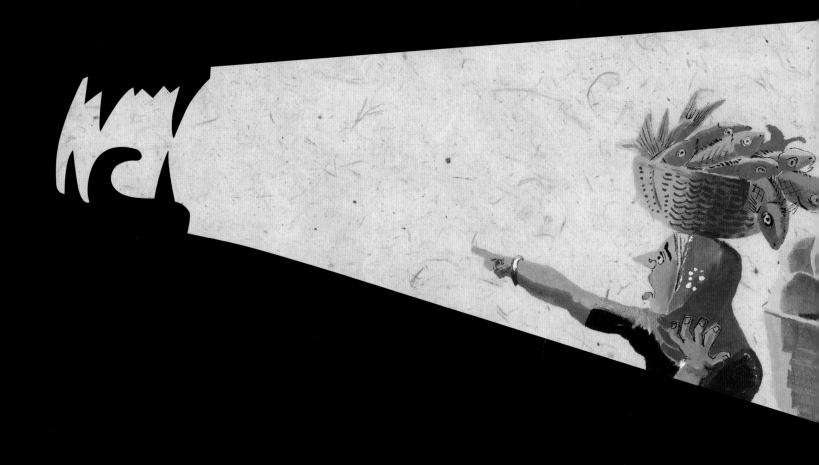

Then the cat opened his mouth in a great yawn and his
belly was flooded with light.

The crabs saw the problem and they wasted no time . . .

. . .cutting a hole—*snip, snip, snip*—with their claws in the belly of the greedy cat.

And when the hole was big enough,
out skittered the crabs,
out walked the sultan
    carrying his bride,
out marched the soldiers
    leading the elephant,
out rode the farmer
    on his donkey,
out stormed the nosy old woman
    scolding the cat soundly,
and last of all, out flew the parrot
    with a little cake in each claw.

"What kind of friend are you?" squawked the parrot to the cat.

"I'm sorry," said the cat. "I'll never be greedy again."

So the parrot, feeling a little bit sorry for his old friend, brought a needle and thread to him, and the cat spent the rest of the day sewing up the big hole in his belly.